Bear about Town

L'Ours dans la ville

Stella Blackstone
Debbie Harter

Bear goes to town
every day.

L'Ours va en ville
tous les jours.

He likes to walk
all the way.

Il aime faire
toute la route à pied.

**On Monday,
he goes to the bakery.**

Le lundi,
il va à la boulangerie.

On Tuesday,
he goes for a swim.

**Le mardi,
il va nager.**

On Wednesday,
he watches a film.

Retrouve les endroits où l'Ours va chaque jour.

Vocabulary / Vocabulaire

Monday – lundi
Tuesday – mardi
Wednesday – mercredi
Thursday – jeudi
Friday – vendredi
Saturday – samedi
Sunday – dimanche

Barefoot Books
124 Walcot Street
Bath, BA1 5BG, UK

Barefoot Books
2067 Massachusetts Ave
Cambridge, MA 02140, USA

Translated by Servane Champion

First published in Great Britain by Barefoot Books Ltd in 2000 and in the United States of America by Barefoot Books Inc in 2000. This edition published in 2010

This book has been printed in China by Hung Hing Off-set Printing Ltd on 100% acid-free paper

ISBN 978-1-84686-376-9

1 3 5 7 9 8 6 4 2

British Cataloguing-in-Publication Data:
a catalogue record for this book is available from the British Library

Library of Congress Cataloging-in-Publication Data is available upon request

Le mercredi,
il regarde un film.

On Thursday,
he visits the gym.

Le jeudi,
il va au gymnase.

**On Friday,
he goes to the toyshop.**

**Le vendredi,
il va au magasin de jouets.**

**On Saturday,
he strolls through the park.**

Le samedi,
il se promène dans le parc.

On Sunday,
he goes to the playground,

**Le dimanche,
il va à l'aire de jeux,**

And plays with his friends until dark.

Et il joue avec ses amis jusqu'à la nuit.

Find the places Bear visits each day.